Happy Reading
John Robbins

N/A

D1591687

DISCARD

The Tooth Fairy
IS BROKE

Written by John Robbins
Illustrated by Rae Owings

CLARK-DAVIS
PUBLISHING CO.
Darnestown, Maryland

ISBN # 0-945938-01-2

Text copyright © 1981 by John N. Robbins, Jr.
Illustrations copyright © 1988 by Rae Owings
All Rights Reserved
Published in the United States by
Clark-Davis Publishing Co.
12551 Carrington Hill Drive
Darnestown, Md. 20878-2240

Editor: Courtenay Gemmill
Design: Dave Pfeiffer

This book was typeset and printed by
Presstar Printing Corp. of Silver Spring, Md.

Library of Congress Catalog Card Number 88-063141
ISBN # 0-945938-01-2

10   9   8   7   6   5   4   3   2   1

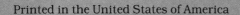

Printed in the United States of America

Myrtle, the tooth fairy was upset. She was worse than upset. She was distressed, depressed and dejected. It wasn't because she had lost her fairy crown. She was always losing her crown. It wasn't because her tutu was tattered. Her tutu was always tattered. It wasn't even because her feet hurt.

No. Myrtle was upset because she was broke.
All the years of putting money under the
pillow of every child who had lost a
tooth had finally taken all she had.
First it had been nickles, then
dimes and then, with inflation,
even a quarter had not been
enough. Her money was
gone, so now what was
she going to do?

Myrtle looked at her
list for this evening's calls.

There were 78 in New York,

104 in Los Angeles,

The list went on and on . . . hundreds of children who would wake up tomorrow morning and expect at least a quarter or two under the pillow. There was nothing to do but pay a visit to Oberon, king of the fairies. That in itself was a task, for the trip to the royal glen was long and tiresome. If she caught Oberon in a bad mood, it would all be for nothing.

Myrt sighed. There was no other solution, so she set out for Oberon's castle.

Being somewhat overweight, Myrt didn't fly with the ease and grace of the other fairies. She rather bumped along, hoping that traffic wouldn't be too bad and that her fragile wings wouldn't break.

After many hours, she arrived at the royal glen. Several familiar faces greeted her—Sam the sandman, Cupid, Bluebird, Robin Goodfellow, Jack Frost and others.

"Myrt, you look bad!" said Cupid, "Trouble?".

"Trouble?! Look, I've got 7,432 calls tonight and not one penny. There will be 7,432 disappointed children tomorrow if I don't get some money from somewhere."

"That's the problem with you cash fairies," said the sandman. "All I give is peaceful sleep and it doesn't cost me a thing. How did you ever get yourself into the money business in the first place?"

"Yes," agreed Bluebird. "You should give happiness as I do. Happiness is free, so I never run short. I just put in an appearance, and people look and say — 'There's the bluebird of happiness,' and suddenly their day is brightened. Just like that."

"Look," said Myrtle, "it's tradition. I don't know how it started. I inherited the job from my mother, who inherited it from her mother! It's my job and I do it. I have to!"

With that she flew on, hoping to catch
King Oberon before his nap time.
   When Myrtle arrived at the castle,
Oberon was still on his throne but he
was nodding off, his head drooping
to one side. Soon he would be sound
asleep. His majestic robes and
enormous size made Myrtle feel very
small indeed.
   "Uh hum," said Myrt. "Uh HUM,"
a little louder. "Excuse me,
Your Majesty, but . . ."

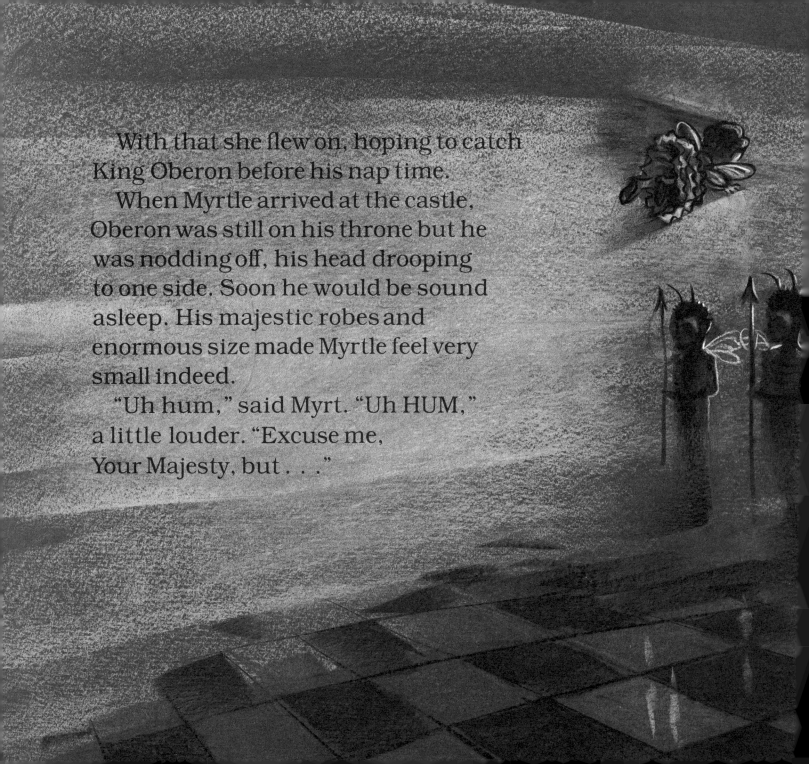

"Whatever it is — NO!" roared Oberon waking with a start. "Absolutely NOT. Impossible. Can't be done. Now go away. I'm tired!" He pounded his scepter for emphasis, startling poor Myrtle, but she would not be put off.

"But it's an emergency!"

"What sort of emergency?"

"I'm broke!"

"Broke?!"

"Yes, I haven't a penny, and there will be 7,432 disappointed children tomorrow morning if I don't find some money."

"Who are you?"

"Myrtle the . . ."

"Tooth fairy. Ah, yes. Now I remember. Gotta take off some weight, Myrt."

"Yes, sir."

"And clean up the costume."

"Yes, sir."

"Where's your crown?"

"I lost it."

"Find it. *Dismissed.*"

"But — you must help me. I need money." Myrt was pleading now. "Please."

"I don't have any money."

"Well then, who does?"

Oberon creased his brow and seemed to be deep in thought. Myrtle waited impatiently while Oberon thought. A curious expression crossed his face — a worried frown. He remembered something.

"I doubt this is any *real* solution but — no, no, it's too dangerous."

"What's too dangerous? I'm desperate. I'll do anything."

"No, I couldn't suggest THEM."

"Who's THEM?"

"The Trolls. The Gutter Trolls."

"Oh, dear. I've heard of them."

"No doubt you have, and if you're wise, you'll have nothing to do with them."

"But . . . do they have money?"

"Dear Myrt. They have money, but nothing could make me go there. Not even . . . DIRE NEED!"

"But this is MORE than dire need. It's a catastrophe. I must go!"

"Well," he warned, "if you do go, be certain you go in the daytime. By no means stay among them past sunset, for there is nothing, NOTHING so awful as a gutter troll at NIGHT."

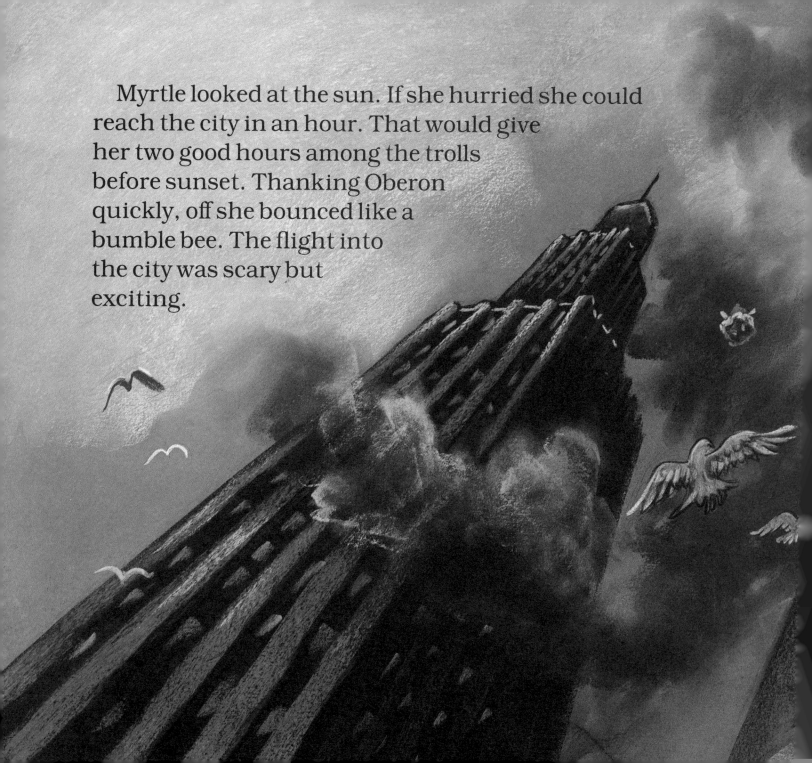

Myrtle looked at the sun. If she hurried she could reach the city in an hour. That would give her two good hours among the trolls before sunset. Thanking Oberon quickly, off she bounced like a bumble bee. The flight into the city was scary but exciting.

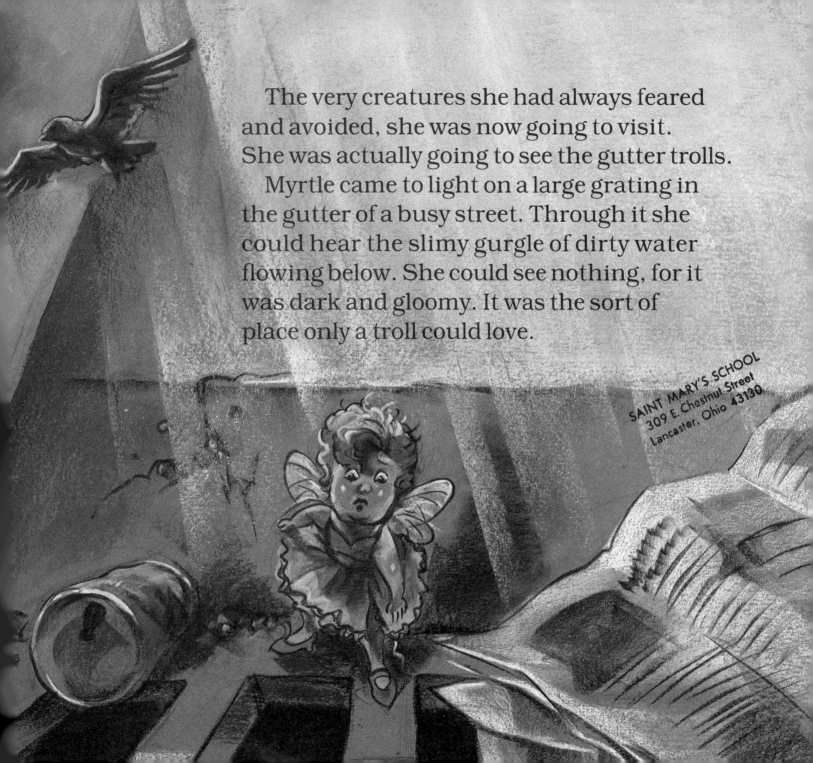

The very creatures she had always feared
and avoided, she was now going to visit.
She was actually going to see the gutter trolls.
    Myrtle came to light on a large grating in
the gutter of a busy street. Through it she
could hear the slimy gurgle of dirty water
flowing below. She could see nothing, for it
was dark and gloomy. It was the sort of
place only a troll could love.

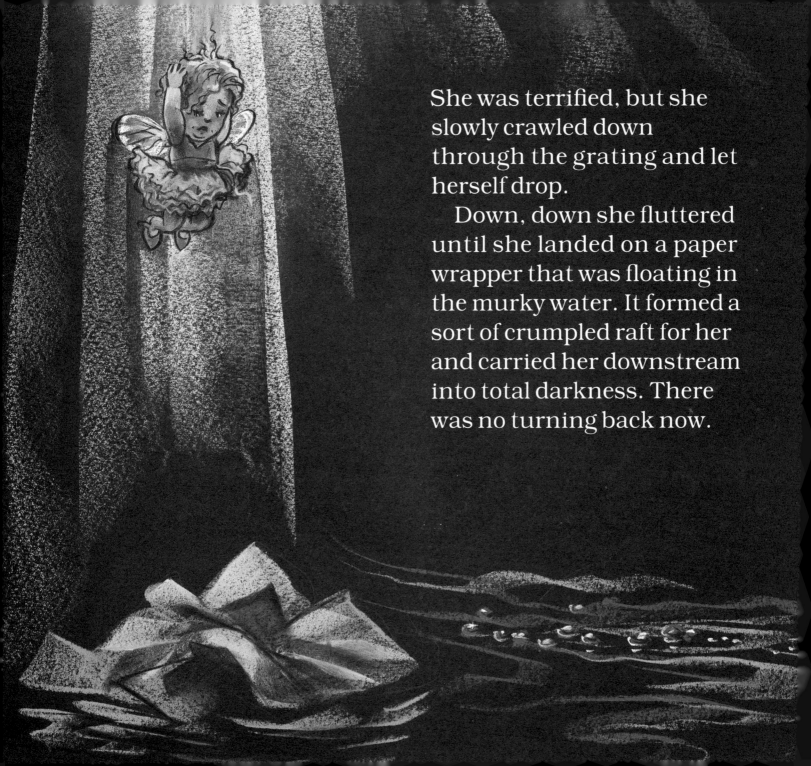

She was terrified, but she slowly crawled down through the grating and let herself drop.

Down, down she fluttered until she landed on a paper wrapper that was floating in the murky water. It formed a sort of crumpled raft for her and carried her downstream into total darkness. There was no turning back now.

After awhile the stream widened, and the current slowed, and Myrtle found herself in a large cavern. On one side she could make out a ledge. Here and there, large rats with glistening, red eyes glared hungrily at her. They moved soundlessly as they watched her and waited.

Then she heard it. Soft at first but then more distinct. It was a low, whispery laughter — a wet laughter. "He, he, ha, ha." The trolls.

As her paper raft drifted toward the ledge, she saw a door. It was wooden with large, rusty hinges and an iron latch. Below the latch was a keyhole.

Her raft drew nearer. The laughter grew louder. "He, he, ha, ha."

Bump! She had reached the ledge. Carefully she stepped off the raft onto the ledge. Then she peeked through the keyhole. Inside she could make out a large room. It was quite beautiful. A gold chandelier hung in the center. Rich, red wallpaper was dotted here and there with gilded sconces. A big, carved wooden table was surrounded by several ornate chairs with red velvet cushions.

Suddenly the laughter came again, and a troll appeared. She was not prepared for anything quite so ugly. Its whole head seemed to be a nose, all bent and warted. Beady, red eyes were almost hidden by black, bushy brows, and small, round ears stuck out on either side near the top.

Below the head, coarse, black fur grew in all directions. Out of the fur grew skinny, pink arms and bony, pink legs that ended in enormous feet.

The troll carried an elegant silver platter and placed it on the table.

It was a meal — perhaps someone's dinner. The troll was joined by another, almost identical one. Then a third. The second and third trolls carried wine goblets and silver pitchers. All of these were placed on the table. Everything grew silent. Then suddenly, through the keyhole, Myrtle saw all three turn toward her.

The first
troll spoke.
The voice sounded dead —
dry and dead.
"She who would peep . . .

. . . might be good to eat."
"Yes — yes," agreed the other two.
"A visitor unbeckoned."
"Shall we ask her in?"
"Into the pot — why not?"
Myrtle looked about.
Her raft had drifted away.
Her wings were frozen in fear.
She had no escape.

Suddenly the door flew open, and she was seized. Cold, bony fingers clasped all about her, and she was whisked into the room and dropped roughly onto the large table. She trembled at the looks on the three horrible faces which now glared at her.

"Spy!" shouted one.

"Oberon's spy from goodie-goodie land!"

"Did you think we would not catch you? FOOL!"

Myrtle tried to speak.

"Please, I have not come to spy! I have come to visit as a friend."

"Did you hear her? A friend indeed. A fat, little do-good fairy."

"You will never see the daylight again, for now you must deal with—HOGARD!"

"Hogard?"

"Do not speak his name! You have no right to speak his name! Do you understand?"

"I'm sorry."

"She's sorry. She's sorry. Ha, ha, he, he."

"I am truly sorry. I came to see . . ."

"You may call him BEAUTY."

"Beauty. Yes, I came to see . . . uh . . . Beauty." The three trolls were silent. They looked at one another, then slowly they backed away. One by one they disappeared from the room.

Myrtle was left all alone.
She nervously glanced
about the room. It was truly
marvelous. The trolls, for all
their ugliness, had
surrounded themselves
with the loveliest of things.
Gold and satin — velvet and
silver were everywhere.

The room was still.

She waited.

A chime struck
somewhere. Then the
strings of a harp whispered
a beautiful chord . . .

. . . and a door at the end of the hall opened.

Through it stepped the most frightening creature she had ever imagined.

It moved toward her in a menacing way. A frog-like head with horns wobbled on a skinny neck. Below, all was covered by a robe of purple silk. Where hands should have stuck from the sleeves, there were horrible claws.

It came closer.

It slowly began to circle the table, never taking its eyes off Myrtle. Then with one of its horrible claws, it reached out and touched her and laughed deeply and softly.

Myrtle was terrified. She could not move. Why had she ever dared to come to this awful place? These hideous creatures!

At last it sat at the head of the table and looked at her with a hungry squint of the eyes. It spoke: "You're a nice, plump fairy."

Myrtle drew in her breath and tried to be smaller.

"You're a **very** nice, plump fairy."

Myrtle had to think fast. She had to use her words carefully to get out of this alive.

"You must be BEAUTY."

It did not respond.

Myrtle went on, "I must say that I have never seen such a lovely place. The furnishings are extraordinary. You have very fine taste . . . Oh, and I couldn't help admiring your eyes."

Suddenly there was a change of expression . . .

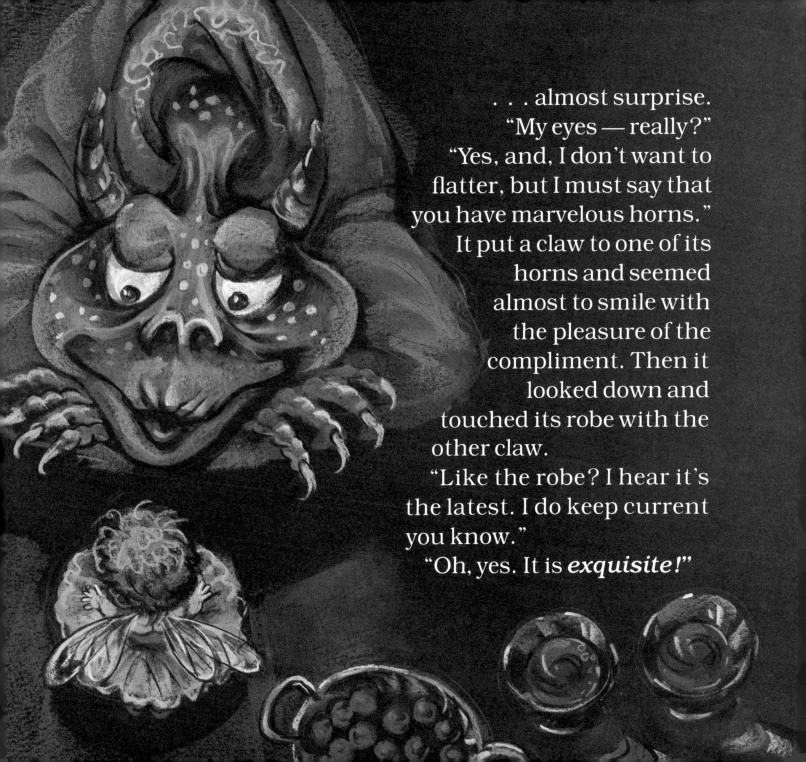

. . . almost surprise.
"My eyes — really?"
"Yes, and, I don't want to flatter, but I must say that you have marvelous horns." It put a claw to one of its horns and seemed almost to smile with the pleasure of the compliment. Then it looked down and touched its robe with the other claw.
"Like the robe? I hear it's the latest. I do keep current you know."
"Oh, yes. It is *exquisite!*"

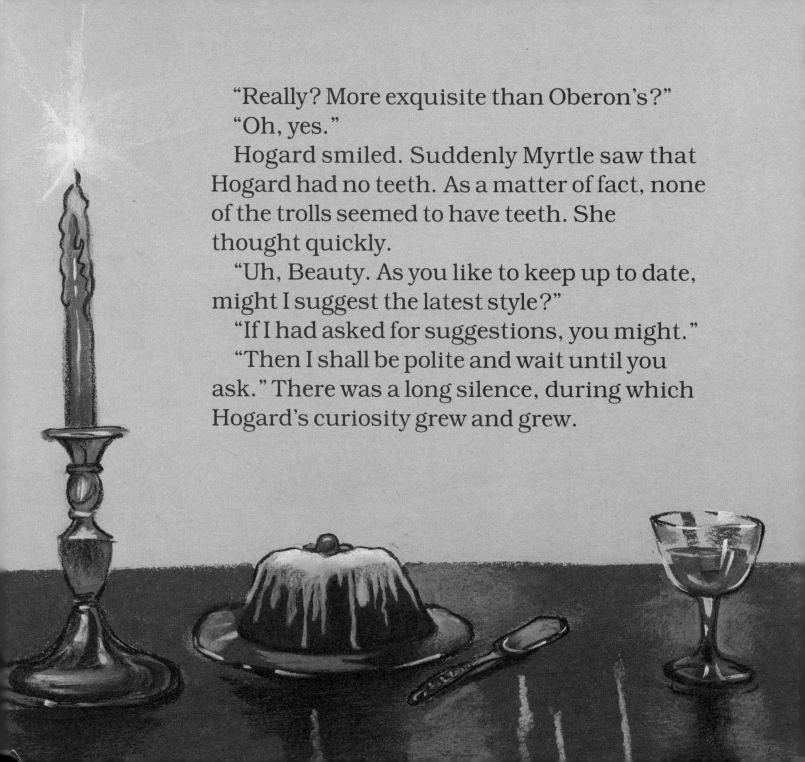

"Really? More exquisite than Oberon's?"

"Oh, yes."

Hogard smiled. Suddenly Myrtle saw that Hogard had no teeth. As a matter of fact, none of the trolls seemed to have teeth. She thought quickly.

"Uh, Beauty. As you like to keep up to date, might I suggest the latest style?"

"If I had asked for suggestions, you might."

"Then I shall be polite and wait until you ask." There was a long silence, during which Hogard's curiosity grew and grew.

He could stand it
no longer.
"WHAT IS IT?
WHAT IS IT!!!?"

"Teeth." Myrtle smiled, and it must be admitted here that she did have perfect teeth.

Hogard looked closely, then put his claw to his toothless gum.

"Teeth," he murmured.

"Yes. They give that extra sparkle to your smile. Not to mention, they also help in eating . . . chewing you know."

"Ah, yes. I can see how they could. How does one get TEETH?"

"I sell them."

"Oh, really. How much?"

"Cheap. 50¢ each. Of course, you would want them also for all the other trolls who serve you so faithfully."

"Well, of course."

"Then you would need quite a few, but I think my supply is ample. I shall be getting in quite a few tonight, 7,432 to be exact. That could get you started. Then each morning starting tomorrow, I could deliver more."

"And you're sure it's not just a passing fad?"

"Oh, no. Teeth are here to stay. I can safely say that."
"Then it's a deal. 7,432 teeth, that comes to $3,716.00.
I hope you can take it in coins. You see, that's all we
usually find in the gutter."

"Oh, coins would be perfect."

Myrtle wondered if night had fallen. There was no way of knowing down here, and she well remembered Oberon's warning: "By no means stay among them past sunset, for there is nothing, NOTHING so awful as a gutter troll at night!"

She quickly added, "If I could get the money right now, I could be sure of having the teeth here by morning."

"That's easy." Hogard rapped twice upon the table and the three trolls appeared.

"Bring the money chest and escort our lovely fairy to the light. Tomorrow I shall have a nice surprise for all of you."

"Yes, your beauty."

So, Myrtle found herself wealthy once more.
She couldn't help feeling somewhat
pleased with herself. After all, she had solved
her problem.

From now on she would have plenty of
money, and the trolls . . .

. . . well, they would have teeth.